TRICKY
TORTOISE

Also by Mwenye Hadithi and Adrienne Kennaway

Greedy Zebra
Hot Hippo
Crafty Chameleon

First edition

Library of Congress Cataloging-in-Publication Data
Mwenye Hadithi.
    Tricky Tortoise.
    Summary: Tortoise outsmarts Elephant by proving he
can jump right over the elephant's "tiny and stupid" head.
    [1. Turtles—Fiction. 2. Elephants—Fiction.
3. Africa—Fiction] I. Moore, Adrienne, 1945–   ill.
II. Title.
PZ7.M975Tr 1988   [E]   88-9220
ISBN 0-316-33724-2

10 9 8 7 6 5 4 3 2 1

Printed in Belgium

TRICKY TORTOISE

by **Mwenye Hadithi**

Illustrated by **Adrienne Kennaway**

Little, Brown and Company
Boston   Toronto

When Tortoise was asleep,
he looked like a round rock.
The other animals sometimes
trod on him by mistake.

When Elephant
trod on him for the three hundred
and thirty-second time, he was very
angry, for his shell had already been mended
so many times that it looked like a coat of patches.

"Listen, Elephant!" he called out. "You be more careful. You seem to think you're the most important animal in the forest!"

"Well, I am!" said Elephant, who was drinking in the river. He was very big-headed, and stuffed full of self-importance as well. "Yes I am. And I'm bigger than anyone else, too!"

"But what about your silly head?" Tortoise laughed. "Have you ever seen your head?"

Elephant tried to see his own head, turning his eyes this way and that. "Umm, well no…" he said, and his eyes crossed from trying. "Nobody can see his own head. But I can see bits of it, like the tip of my nose."

"Well, your head is so tiny and stupid, I bet I could jump right over it," said the cross Tortoise.
"You could not," laughed Elephant. "Go ahead and try! I bet you can't jump over my head."

"Today I'm too tired," said Tortoise, and he yawned. "But be here tomorrow at daybreak and then I bet I can jump over your silly little head. And the loser of the bet will pay for a huge feast at which the winner will be a most important guest. Agreed?"

"Agreed," laughed Elephant, shooting water out of his trunk and nearly drowning the small rabbits drinking by the river.

The next day, while the sun was not yet risen, Tortoise arrived at the place with his brother, who looked exactly like Tortoise himself. Tortoise told his brother to hide in a pile of leaves by the road. When Elephant arrived, he found Tortoise doing exercises. All the forest animals knew how clever Tortoise could be and, when they heard about the bet and the feast, they came to watch the fun and see what trick he would play on Elephant.

When Elephant came to the spot where Tortoise's brother was hidden, Tortoise himself called out: "Ah. There you are! Now, just stand there and we'll begin. Ready? Yes? *Weyo weeyo wee... yo... HUP we go!*" and Tortoise suddenly hid his legs and his head and his tail under his shell, disguising himself as a rock, just as his brother called:

"Down we come! Easy, easy!" on the other side of Elephant. Elephant looked around, surprised. Tortoise had jumped over his head! He must have, for there he was… And then Tortoise's brother cried: "*Weyo weeyo wee … yo … HUP we go!*"

Elephant turned
his head again,
surprised and very cross to see
Tortoise back down on the ground, on the other side of him,
shouting, "Down we come! Easy, easy! Shall I do it again?
Weyo weeyo wee... yo... HUP we go!" Tortoise called
as he became a rock again. "Down we come! Easy, easy!"
called Tortoise's brother, popping out from under the leaves.

"Tortoise wins! Tortoise wins!"
yelled all the other animals.

Elephant patted his head with his trunk to see how really very small it was.

"See, Elephant," said Tortoise, "you may be big, but that isn't everything. Why, even I can jump over your head. Shall I do it again?"

"No, no!" Elephant said crossly. "You win, you win!"

And all the animals went off to the feast,
laughing and carrying Tortoise high in the air,
for he was a most important guest.

And Elephant sat feeling certain that
he had been made to look foolish,
and he didn't like feeling foolish at all.

But since that day he has been very careful
not to step on Tortoise again.

MWE   Mwenye, Hadithi
             Tricky Tortoise

$13.45

DATE			